RNER

Silly Sadie, Silly Samuel

For Sue Alexander, Erica Silverman, and Karen Winnick,
three very wise friends —A. W. P.

For Darlene and Harold —S. W.

Text copyright © 2000 by Ann Whitford Paul
Illustrations copyright © 2000 by Sylvie Wickstrom

Simon & Schuster Books for Young Readers
An imprint of Simon & Schuster Children's Publishing Division
1230 Avenue of the Americas
New York, NY 10020

READY-TO-READ is a registered trademark of
Simon & Schuster, Inc.
The text for this book was set in Utopia.
Printed and bound in the United States of America
10 9 8 7 6 5 4 3 2 1

Library of Congress Cataloging-in-Publication Data
Paul, Ann Whitford.
Silly Sadie, silly Samuel / by Ann Whitford Paul ; illustrated by
Sylvie Wickstrom.
p. cm. — (Ready-to-read)
Summary: Although their actions sometimes seem silly
to their sensible neighbor, Sadie and Samuel enjoy their
nonsensical lives.
ISBN 0-689-81689-8 (hc.)
[1. Humorous stories.] I. Wickstrom, Sylvie, ill. II. Title.
III. Series.
PZ7.P278338Si 1998
[E]--dc21 97-25146
CIP AC

Table of Contents

Washing Samuel's Overalls

Sadie and her husband Samuel
were eating pancakes.
"I need more syrup," Samuel said.
He reached across the table.
His arm bumped his plate.
The plate fell in his lap.

"What a mess!" Samuel cried.
"My overalls are all sticky."
"Come with me," Sadie said.
She led him out to the well.
Sadie pulled up a bucket of water.
She poured it over Samuel.

"This will not take long,"
she said.
She rubbed some soap on Samuel.
Bubbles covered him
from head to foot.

Just then, their neighbor Hazel
walked by.
"Sadie! What are you doing?"
she asked.
"I am washing Samuel's overalls,"
Sadie answered.
"And I am having a wonderful
bath," said Samuel.

Painting the Fence

"Today I will paint
our fence," Samuel said.
He opened a pail of white paint.
He painted one picket white.
"This is too plain," he said.
Samuel mixed up some
yellow paint.
He painted one picket yellow.
"That is better," he said.

Then he mixed up some
green paint.
He painted one picket green.
Next Samuel mixed up some
red paint.
He painted one picket red.
"This fence is looking so pretty,"
he said.
Samuel painted one picket blue.
He painted one picket orange
and one purple and one pink.

Just then, Sadie and Hazel
returned from the village.
"Oh, dear. Oh, dear!"
Hazel said.
"Look at what Samuel has done
to your fence."
Sadie smiled.
"Yes," she said.
"He has painted me a lovely
rainbow."

The Argument

Samuel pounded a nail
into the wall.
He hung up a new picture.
Sadie took down the picture.
"That is not right," she said.
She hung the picture up again
in the same place.
"It looks much better here,"
she said.

"No," said Samuel.
He took down the picture
and put it right back.
"The picture belongs HERE,"
he shouted.
Sadie yanked down the picture.
She hung it back up.
"NO! HERE!" she shouted.
Hazel hurried over to their house.
"Why are you shouting?"
she asked.

"I think the picture belongs HERE,"
Samuel said.
"NO! The picture belongs HERE!"
Sadie shouted.
"NO! HERE!" shouted Samuel.
"NO! HERE!" shouted Sadie.

Hazel ran between them.
"Stop it!" she cried.
Samuel looked at Hazel.
"Pay no mind to us," he said.
"We are just having an argument."
Hazel shook her head.
"But this is a strange argument.
You are both hanging the picture
in the same place."
Samuel hugged Sadie.
"We are having the best kind of
argument," he said.
"Yes," Sadie agreed.
"When we stop arguing,
we will *both* be right."

A New Quilt

Samuel was carving a duck
out of wood.
Sadie sat nearby.
She was cutting Samuel's good
Sunday shirt into small squares.
She cut his good Sunday suit
into small squares, too.
Then Sadie got out
her needle and thread.
She started sewing.

After a long time, Hazel tapped
at the window.
"What are you doing, Sadie?"
she asked.
"I am making a quilt for our bed,"
Sadie said.
She held it up for Hazel to see.
Hazel pointed to a square.
"That looks like Samuel's good
Sunday shirt," she said.
"It *is* Samuel's good Sunday shirt,"
Sadie said.

Hazel pointed to another square.
"That looks like Samuel's
Sunday suit."
"You are right," Sadie answered.
"Oh, no," Hazel cried.
"You have ruined Samuel's
good Sunday clothes!"

"Why are you raising your voice?"
asked Sadie.
"Samuel wore these clothes only
on Sunday."
Samuel nodded.
"Sadie is right," he said.
He took the quilt from Sadie and
wrapped it around his shoulders.
Then Samuel said, "When Sadie is
done sewing, I can sleep under
this quilt *every* night."

Finding Sadie's Ring

Sadie went out to the barn
to give the horse a carrot.
Her ring slipped off her finger.
It dropped on the floor.
Ping!
Sadie got down
on her hands and knees.
Back and forth she crawled.
"I cannot find my ring,"
she moaned.
Samuel stopped milking the cow.
"The light is better outside,"
he said. "Come with me.
I will help you look for your ring."

Sadie and Samuel went outside.
They both got down on their
hands and knees.
They crawled back and forth.
Just then, Hazel came over.
"What are you doing?"
Hazel asked.
"My ring fell off in the barn,"
Sadie said.
"We are looking for it."
"Why are you looking out here?"
Hazel asked.
"The light is not good in the barn,"
Samuel said.

Hazel shook her head.
She went into her house and came
out with a lantern.
"You need to take light *inside* the
barn," she said.

Sadie and Samuel followed Hazel
to the barn.
"There is my ring!" Sadie cried.
"We are lucky to have such a wise
neighbor," Samuel said.

Good Night, Hazel

Sadie, Samuel, and Hazel sat
together on the porch.
They looked at the moon and stars.
They talked.
Finally, Hazel stood up.
"It is time for me to go," she said.
"Goodnight, Hazel," Sadie said.

Hazel waved goodbye.
"I will see you in the morning,"
she said.
"Yes," Sadie said.
"We will get up
after the lion roars."
"You mean after the rooster
crows," Hazel said.

Sadie stretched and yawned.
"No," she answered.
"I mean *after the lion roars.*"
"But you do not have
a lion on your farm," Hazel said.
Samuel patted Sadie's hand.

"Well, then," he said.
"I guess we will have to sleep
all morning long."